Young Bandit

Young Animal Pride Series
Book 14

Cataloging-in-Publication Data

Sargent, Dave, 1941--
    Young bandit / by Dave and Pat Sargent ;
illustrated by Elaine Woodword.—Prairie Grove, AR :
Ozark Publishing, c2005.
    p. cm. (Young animal pride series ; 14)

    "I help others"—Cover.
    SUMMARY: When a young weasel family
loses its mother and father in an accident,
Bandit takes charge and feeds his family
with the help of Farmer John and Barney.
    ISBN 1-56763-889-9 (hc)
          1-56763-890-2 (pbk)

    1. Weasels—Juvenile fiction.
[1. Weasels—Fiction.] I. Sargent, Pat, 1936–
II. Woodword, Elaine, 1956– ill. III. Title.
IV. Series.

    PZ10.3.S243Ba 2005
    [Fic]—dc21   2004093000

Printed in the United States of America

Young Bandit

Young Animal Pride Series
Book 14

by Dave and Pat Sargent

Illustrated by Elaine Woodword

Ozark Publishing, Inc.
P.O. Box 228
Prairie Grove, AR 72753

Dave and Pat Sargent, authors of the extremely popular Animal Pride Series, visit schools all over the United States, free of charge. If you would like to have Dave and Pat visit your school, please ask your librarian to call 1-800-321-5671.

Foreword

Bandit takes care of his five brothers and sisters after their parents die in a rock slide. Farmer John and Barney the Bear Killer help him.

1

My name is Bandit.

I am a weasel.

Mama and Daddy died.

Rocks fell on them.

I learned to hunt.

I caught grasshoppers.

I caught crickets.

I fed my brothers and sisters.

Farmer John saw us.

Barney saw us.

I went to the chicken house.

Farmer John had left eggs.

The eggs were for me.

I fed my family.

Barney guarded the eggs.

Farmer John told him to.

Sammy Skunk came by.

Barney chased him away.

Barney is my friend.